FERGUS AND ZEKE
AT THE SCIENCE FAIR

KATE MESSNER

ILLUSTRATED BY HEATHER ROSS

CANDLEWICK PRESS

FOR MEGHAN AND MICHELLE
K. M.

FOR BEE AND THE MICE
H. R.

Text copyright © 2018 by Kate Messner
Illustrations copyright © 2018 by Heather Ross

Candlewick Sparks®. Candlewick Sparks is a registered trademark of Candlewick Press, Inc.

First paperback edition 2019

Library of Congress Catalog Card Number 2018959540
ISBN 978-0-7636-7847-0 (hardcover)
ISBN 978-1-5362-0899-3 (paperback)

19 20 21 22 23 24 CCP 10 9 8 7 6 5 4 3 2

Printed in Shenzhen, Guangdong, China

This book was typeset in Minion.
The illustrations were created digitally.

Candlewick Press
99 Dover Street
Somerville, Massachusetts 02144

visit us at www.candlewick.com

CONTENTS

CHAPTER 1
PLANTING SEEDS
- 1 -

CHAPTER 2
RACE THROUGH THE MAZE!
- 11 -

CHAPTER 3
TRAINING LUCY
- 21 -

CHAPTER 4
SCIENCE FAIR DAY!
- 31 -

CHAPTER 1
PLANTING SEEDS

FERGUS AND ZEKE loved being the class pets in Miss Maxwell's room. Everything the children did, Fergus and Zeke did, too. They listened at storytime . . . painted masterpieces in art class . . . and kept their own special calendar and journal.

One day, Miss Maxwell made an announcement. "Our school is having a science fair," she said. "Everyone will make a project or do an experiment, and in two weeks, we will invite the science fair judges and our families to see our work."

"Cool!" said Emma. "I'm going to make a model of the solar system."

"I'm going to do an experiment with plants," said Will. "I'll find out how they grow best."

"I want to do a project with animals," said Lucy. "But I'm not sure what my experiment will be."

Fergus and Zeke wanted to be in the science fair, too. But they weren't sure what to do either.

The next day, Will planted bean seeds in little cups of dirt. He gave them each a drink of water. Then he put one cup in the middle of the classroom. He put one cup by the window. He put a third cup in the coat closet.

"It is very dark in there," Fergus said. "Plants need light. I do not think that plant will grow."

"Our cage is nice and sunny. We should do a plant experiment, too," said Zeke. So he and Fergus buried three sunflower seeds.

They watered the seeds.

They watched and waited all day long.

All that watching and waiting made them hungry.

"I do not think we are the right scientists for this experiment," Fergus said. "Maybe we should do an experiment like Neela's instead."

Neela had a big box full of sand. She was studying erosion, learning how soil can be worn away by wind or water. When Neela blew on the sand, it moved across the box. When she poured water on it, the water pushed the sand aside.

"That's a great idea!" Zeke said. "You make a pile of wood chips. I will climb to the top of the wheel and pour water on them. Then you can observe and write down what happens."

So Fergus piled up the wood chips.

Zeke carried their water dish to the very tip-top of the wheel.

"Ready to observe?" Zeke called.

"Ready!" Fergus answered.

"Oh dear," Zeke said. "I am sorry, Fergus."

"I observe that you do not have very good aim," Fergus said. He felt soggy and sad.

How could they be in the science fair without a project?

CHAPTER 2
RACE THROUGH THE MAZE!

The next week, Lucy brought in a flat cardboard box with more cardboard inside. The inside pieces made a twisty path all over the box.

"Hello, mice!" Lucy brought the box to their cage. "Look what I made for you! It took me a long time, but doesn't it look great? I am going to train you to run through this maze for the science fair. We only have a few days to practice, so let's get started!"

Fergus jumped up. "Did you hear that, Zeke? We are going to be in the science fair after all!"

But Zeke was not happy. "I want to *do* an experiment," he said. "I do not want to *be* an experiment." He hid in his mad place so Lucy couldn't see him.

Fergus looked around the classroom. All the students were working on their projects.

"The science fair is in just a few days," Miss Maxwell said. "All of your experiments are looking great!"

"Please, Zeke?" Fergus called. "It might be our only chance to be in the science fair. And you have to admit, that maze looks like fun."

Zeke poked his head out from his mad place to see.

"Watch me!" Fergus ran to the edge of the cage. Lucy scooped him up and put him in the cardboard maze box.

Fergus sniffed and skittered. He hurried
through the maze. It wasn't very hard.

UP

Lucy did a bouncy cheer for him. "Go! Go! Go, Fergus, go!"

When Fergus got to the end, Lucy said, "Good job!" She gave him a mouse treat.

"Come on, Zeke!" Fergus called. "It's fun! And Lucy gave me a treat at the end."

Zeke came out from his mad place, and Lucy put him in the maze. But Zeke did not follow the path. He climbed over the walls to the end and waited for his treat.

Lucy picked him up and frowned. She put him back at the beginning. "You cheated," she said. "You have to follow the path."

"Not fair," Zeke grumped. But this time he followed the path.

Lucy did her bouncy cheer. "Go! Go! Go, Zeke, go!"

And Zeke got a mouse treat at the end.

Fergus and Zeke raced through the maze again and again. Lucy cheered and gave them treat after treat.

"This is a good project," Fergus said after Lucy put them back in their cage.

"Yes," Zeke agreed. "But I still think we should be the ones doing the experiment."

"Where would we find animals to train?" Fergus said.

"Are children animals?" Zeke asked.

"I think so," Fergus said. "But I hear Miss Maxwell say the same things to them over and over. They seem very hard to train."

"There's only one way to find out," Zeke said. "We will have to do an experiment."

QUIET TIME!

CHAPTER 3
TRAINING LUCY

The next morning Miss Maxwell told the class, "I hope you have been working hard on your science fair projects."

"My plants are growing well," Will said. "Except for the one in the closet. I think that is because plants need light to grow."

21

"My erosion demonstration is all ready," Neela said.

"My solar system model is almost done," Emma said.

"I've trained our classroom mice to run in a maze," Lucy said. "They're getting very good at it."

"Excellent!" Miss Maxwell said. "The science fair is on Monday. Let's get to work and make the most of our time."

"Today we will train Lucy," Zeke said. "Here's how it will work. When Lucy puts us in the maze, just sit down. Do not start to go until she does the bouncy cheer."

"What if Lucy never does the bouncy cheer?" Fergus asked.

"Then we will not run the maze," Zeke said. "She will have to learn. It is part of the experiment."

Soon, Lucy came and put Fergus and Zeke in the maze. "Ready, mice?" she asked. "Go ahead." She waited with her timer and notebook.

Fergus and Zeke sat down.

Lucy waited. She tapped the side of the box. Fergus and Zeke did not move.

"Did you forget how to do the maze?" Lucy asked. "Come on. Go!"

Fergus looked up. But Lucy did not do the cheer.

"No cheer, no maze," Zeke reminded him.

Lucy looked at Fergus and tipped her head. "Come on, Fergus," she whispered. "You can do it. Go! Go! Go, Fergus, go!"

"Go!" Zeke cried.

And Fergus went. Lucy cheered him all the way through the maze. She gave him a mouse treat at the end.

Then she looked at Zeke. "Your turn."

Zeke did not go.

"You want me to cheer for you, too? Go, Zeke, go!" Lucy said.

Zeke went. But when he was halfway through the maze, Lucy stopped cheering.

Zeke sat down.

"Hey!" Lucy said. "You didn't finish."

Zeke sat. He waited.

"Keep going. Go on," Lucy said. "Go, Zeke, go! Go, Zeke, go!"

Zeke raced to the end of the maze. Lucy wrote something in her notebook.

She looked at Fergus and Zeke. Then she put them back at the beginning of the maze.

"Go," Lucy said.

Fergus and Zeke sat.

Then Lucy cheered, and they ran through the maze again. Lucy wrote something else down in her notebook. She looked confused.

"Time's up!" said Miss Maxwell. "Have a good weekend, and I'll see you all at the science fair on Monday. The best projects will get ribbons!"

"Do you think we've finished training Lucy?" Fergus said.

"Of course we have," said Zeke. "And we didn't even have to give her treats. I cannot wait for the science fair!"

CHAPTER 4
SCIENCE FAIR DAY!

On the day of the science fair, Neela got
the box of sand ready for her erosion
demonstration.

Emma hung her solar system model from
the ceiling.

Will set his plants in front of a poster that
explained what plants need to grow.

Fergus and Zeke cleaned their faces and smoothed their fur.

"Our experiment is going to be the best!" Zeke said. But Fergus was worried. What if they hadn't trained Lucy well enough? Sometimes the children didn't remember things Miss Maxwell taught them. What if Lucy forgot to cheer?

Lucy brought Fergus and Zeke to a special table she'd set up for their maze box.

"Are you ready, mice?" she asked. "I am going to go see the other projects. I'll be back when it's time for our demonstration."

Fergus and Zeke watched the children and judges go from table to table.

Everyone clapped for Emma's solar system and Neela's erosion demonstration.

They marveled at how tall Will's plant had grown.

They made wall puppets with a second-grader's light-and-shadow experiment.

And squealed when a fourth-grader's chemistry project sent soda shooting up to the ceiling.

Finally, Lucy came back to the maze table, with all the students and families and judges. She looked nervous about having so many people watching.

That made Fergus even more nervous.

"What if Lucy forgets to cheer?" Fergus said.

"Don't worry," Zeke whispered. "We have trained her well."

Lucy picked up Fergus and Zeke and put them at the beginning of the maze. "Ready, mice?"

Fergus and Zeke were ready. They hoped Lucy was ready, too.

"Okay. One, two, three . . . go!" Lucy said. But Lucy did not cheer.

So Fergus and Zeke did not go.

The children waited.

The families waited.

The judges tapped their clipboards.

Fergus looked at Lucy. Lucy looked back at Fergus. Then she looked down at her notebook and smiled. "Come on, mice! You can do it," she whispered. And she clapped her hands. "Go, Fergus, go! Go, Zeke, go!" Lucy cheered and cheered.

So Fergus and Zeke ran through the maze. They raced as fast as they could, all the way to the end.

Everyone clapped. "It worked!" Zeke said.

"Do you think they are clapping for us?" Fergus asked.

"Certainly," Zeke said as Lucy put them back in their cage. "After all, we are the ones who trained her."